THE NATIVE SOIL

THE NATIVE SOIL

by Alan E. Nourse

Before the first ship from Earth made a landing on Venus, there was much speculation about what might be found beneath the cloud layers obscuring that planet's surface from the eyes of all observers.

One school of thought maintained that the surface of Venus was a jungle, rank with hot-house moisture, crawling with writhing fauna and man-eating flowers. Another group contended hotly that Venus was an arid desert of wind-carved sandstone, dry and cruel, whipping dust into clouds that sunlight could never penetrate. Others prognosticated an ocean planet with little or no solid ground at all, populated by enormous serpents waiting to greet the first Earthlings with jaws agape.

But nobody knew, of course. Venus was the planet of mystery.

When the first Earth ship finally landed there, all they found was a great quantity of mud.

There was enough mud on Venus to go all the way around twice, with some left over. It was warm, wet, soggy mud—clinging and tenacious. In some places it was gray, and in other places it was black. Elsewhere it was found to be varying shades of brown, yellow, green, blue and purple. But just the same, it was still mud. The sparse Venusian vegetation grew up out of it; the small Venusian natives lived down in it; the steam rose from it and the rain fell on it, and that, it seemed, was that. The planet of mystery was no longer mysterious. It was just messy. People didn't talk about it any more.

But technologists of the Piper Pharmaceuticals, Inc., R&D squad found a certain charm in the Venusian mud.

They began sending cautious and very secret reports back to the Home Office when they discovered just what, exactly was growing in that Venusian mud besides Venusian natives. The Home Office promptly bought up full exploratory and mining rights to the planet for a price that was a brazen steal, and then in high excitement began pouring millions of dollars into ships and machines bound for the muddy planet. The Board of Directors met hoots of derision with secret smiles as they rubbed their hands together softly. Special crews of psychologists were dispatched to Venus to contact the natives; they returned, exuberant, with test-results that proved the natives were friendly, intelligent, co-operative and resourceful, and the Board of Directors rubbed their hands more eagerly together, and poured more money into the Piper Venusian Installation.

It took money to make money, they thought. Let the fools laugh. They wouldn't be laughing long. After all, Piper Pharmaceuticals, Inc., could recognize a gold mine when they saw one.

They thought.

*

Robert Kielland, special investigator and trouble shooter for Piper Pharmaceuticals, Inc., made an abrupt and intimate acquaintance with the fabulous Venusian mud when the landing craft brought him down on that soggy planet. He had transferred from the great bubble-shaped orbital transport ship to the sleek landing craft an hour before, bored and impatient with the whole proposition. He had no desire whatever to go to Venus. He didn't like mud, and he didn't like frontier projects. There had been nothing in his contract with Piper demanding that he travel to other planets in pursuit of his duties, and he had balked at the assignment. He had even balked at the staggering bonus check they offered him to help him get used to the idea.

It was not until they had convinced him that only his own superior judgment, his razor-sharp mind and his extraordinarily shrewd powers of observation and insight could possibly pull Piper Pharmaceuticals, Inc., out of the mudhole they'd gotten themselves into, that he had reluctantly agreed to go. He wouldn't like a moment of it, but he'd go.

Things weren't going right on Venus, it seemed.

The trouble was that millions were going in and nothing was coming out. The early promise of high production figures had faltered, sagged, dwindled and vanished. Venus was getting to be an expensive project to have around, and nobody seemed to know just why.

Now the pilot dipped the landing craft in and out of the cloud blanket, braking the ship, falling closer and closer to the surface as Kielland watched gloomily from the after port. The lurching billows of clouds made him queasy; he opened his Piper samples case and popped a pill into his mouth. Then he gave his nose a squirt or two with his Piper Rhino-Vac nebulizer, just for good measure. Finally, far below them, the featureless gray surface skimmed by. A sparse scraggly forest of twisted gray foliage sprang up at them.

The pilot sighted the landing platform, checked with Control Tower, and eased up for the final descent. He was a skillful pilot, with many landings on Venus to his credit. He brought the ship up on its tail and sat it down on the landing platform for a perfect three-pointer as the jets rumbled to silence.

Then, abruptly, they sank—landing craft, platform and all.

The pilot buzzed Control Tower frantically as Kielland fought down panic. Sorry, said Control Tower. Something must have gone wrong. They'd have them out in a jiffy. Good lord, no, *don't* blast out again, there were a thousand natives in the vicinity. Just be patient, everything would be all right.

They waited. Presently there were thumps and bangs as grapplers clanged on the surface of the craft. Mud gurgled around them as they were hauled up and out with the sound of a giant sipping soup. A mud-encrusted hatchway flew open, and Kielland stepped down on a flimsy-looking platform below. Four small rodent-like creatures were attached to it by ropes; they heaved with a will and began paddling through the soupy mud dragging the platform and Kielland toward a row of low wooden buildings near some stunted trees.

As the creatures paused to puff and pant, the back half of the platform kept sinking into the mud. When they finally reached comparatively solid ground, Kielland was mud up to the hips, and mad enough to blast off without benefit of landing craft.

THE NATIVE SOIL

He surveyed the Piper Venusian Installation, hardly believing what he saw. He had heard the glowing descriptions of the Board of Directors. He had seen the architect's projections of fine modern buildings resting on water-proof buoys, neat boating channels to the mine sites, fine orange-painted dredge equipment (including the new Piper Axis-Traction Dredges that had been developed especially for the operation). It had sounded, in short, just the way a Piper Installation ought to sound.

But there was nothing here that resembled that. Kielland could see a group of little wooden shacks that looked as though they were ready at a moment's notice to sink with a gurgle into the mud. Off to the right across a mud flat one of the dredges apparently had done just that: a swarm of men and natives were hard at work dragging it up again. Control Tower was to the left, balanced precariously at a slight tilt in a sea of mud.

The Piper Venusian Installation didn't look too much like a going concern. It looked far more like a ghost town in the latter stages of decay.

Inside the Administration shack Kielland found a weary-looking man behind a desk, scribbling furiously at a pile of reports. Everything in the shack was splattered with mud. The crude desk and furniture was smeared; the papers had black speckles all over them. Even the man's face was splattered, his clothing encrusted with gobs of still-damp mud. In a corner a young man was industriously scrubbing down the wall with a large brush.

The man wiped mud off Kielland and jumped up with a gleam of hope in his tired eyes. "Ah! Wonderful!" he cried. "Great to see you, old man. You'll find all the papers and reports in order here, everything ready for you—" He brushed the papers away from him with a gesture of finality. "Louie, get the landing craft pilot and don't let him out of your sight. Tell him I'll be ready in twenty minutes—"

"Hold it," said Kielland. "Aren't you Simpson?"

The man wiped mud off his cheeks and spat. He was tall and graying. "That's right."

"Where do you think you're going?"

"Aren't you relieving me?"

"I am not!"

"Oh, my." The man crumbled behind the desk, as though his legs had just given way. "I don't understand it. They told me—"

"I don't care what they told you," said Kielland shortly. "I'm a trouble shooter, not an administrator. When production figures begin to drop, I find out why. The production figures from this place have never gotten high enough to drop."

"This is supposed to be news to me?" said Simpson.

"So you've got troubles."

"Friend, you're right about that."

"Well, we'll straighten them out," Kielland said smoothly. "But first I want to see the foreman who put that wretched landing platform together."

Simpson's eyes became wary. "Uh—you don't really want to see him?"

"Yes, I think I do. When there's such obvious evidence of incompetence, the time to correct it is now."

"Well—maybe we can go outside and see him."

"We'll see him right here." Kielland sank down on the bench near the wall. A tiny headache was developing; he found a capsule in his samples case and popped it in his mouth.

Simpson looked sad and nodded to the orderly who had stopped scrubbing down the wall. "Louie, you heard the man."

"But boss—"

Simpson scowled. Louie went to the door and whistled. Presently there was a splashing sound and a short, gray creature padded in. His hind feet were four-toed webbed paddles; his legs were long and powerful like a kangaroo's. He was covered with thick gray fur which

9

dripped with thick black mud. He squeaked at Simpson, wriggling his nose. Simpson squeaked back sharply.

Suddenly the creature began shaking his head in a slow, rhythmic undulation. With a cry Simpson dropped behind the desk. The orderly fell flat on the floor, covering his face with his arm. Kielland's eyes widened; then he was sitting in a deluge of mud as the little Venusian shook himself until his fur stood straight out in all directions.

Simpson stood up again with a roar. "I've told them a thousand times if I've told them once—" He shook his head helplessly as Kielland wiped mud out of his eyes. "This is the one you wanted to see."

Kielland sputtered. "Can it talk to you?"

"It doesn't talk, it squeaks."

"Then ask it to explain why the platform it built didn't hold the landing craft."

Simpson began whistling and squeaking at length to the little creature. Its shaggy tail crept between its legs and it hung its head like a scolded puppy.

"He says he didn't know a landing craft was supposed to land on the platform," Simpson reported finally. "He's sorry, he says."

"But hasn't he seen a landing craft before?"

Squeak, squeak. "Oh, yes."

"Wasn't he told what the platform was being made for?"

Squeak, squeak. "Of course."

"Then why didn't the platform stand up?"

Simpson sighed. "Maybe he forgot what it was supposed to be used for in the course of building it. Maybe he never really did understand in the first place. I can't get questions like that across to him with this whistling, and I doubt that you'll ever find out which it was."

"Then fire him," said Kielland. "We'll find some other—"

"Oh, no! I mean, let's not be hasty," said Simpson. "I'd hate to have to fire this one—for a while yet, at any rate."

10

"Why?"

"Because we've finally gotten across to him—at least I *think* we have—just how to take down a dredge tube." Simpson's voice was almost tearful. "It's taken us months to teach him. If we fire him, we'll have to start all over again with another one."

Kielland stared at the Venusian, and then at Simpson. "So," he said finally, "I see."

"No, you don't," Simpson said with conviction. "You don't even begin to see yet. You have to fight it for a few months before you really see." He waved the Venusian out the door and turned to Kielland with burden of ten months' frustration in his voice. "They're *stupid*," he said slowly. "They are so incredibly stupid I could go screaming into the swamp every time I see one of them coming. Their stupidity is positively abysmal."

"Then why use them?" Kielland spluttered.

"Because if we ever hope to mine anything in this miserable mudhole, we've got to use them to do it. There just isn't any other way."

With Simpson leading, they donned waist-high waders with wide, flat silicone-coated pans strapped to the feet and started out to inspect the installation.

A crowd of a dozen or more Venusian natives swarmed happily around them like a pack of hounds. They were in and out of the steaming mud, circling and splashing, squeaking: and shaking. They seemed to be having a real field day.

"Of course," Simpson was saying, "since Number Four dredge sank last week there isn't a whale of a lot of Installation left for you to inspect. But you can see what there is, if you want."

"You mean Number Four dredge is the only one you've got to use?" Kielland asked peevishly. "According to my records you have five Axis-Traction dredges, plus a dozen or more of the old kind."

"Ah!" said Simpson. "Well, Number One had its vacuum chamber corroded out a week after we started using dredging. Ran into a vein of stuff with 15 per cent acid content, and it got chewed up something fierce. Number Two sank without a trace—over there in the swamp someplace." He pointed across the black mud flats to a patch of sickly vegetation. "The Mud-pups know where it is, they think, and I suppose they could go drag it up for us if we dared take the time, but it would lose us a month, and you know the production schedule we've been trying to meet."

"So what about Numbers Three and Five?"

"Oh, we still have them. They won't work without a major overhaul, though."

"Overhaul! They're brand new."

"They *were*. The Mud-pups didn't understand how to sluice them down properly after operations. When this guck gets out into the air it hardens like cement. You ever see a cement mixer that hasn't been cleaned out after use for a few dozen times? That's Numbers Three and Five."

"What about the old style models?"

"Half of them are out of commission, and the other half are holding the islands still."

"Islands?"

"Those chunks of semisolid ground we have Administration built on. The chunk that keeps Control Tower in one place."

"Well, what are they going to do—walk away?"

"That's just about right. The first week we were in operation we kept wondering why we had to travel farther every day to get to the dredges. Then we realized that solid ground on Venus isn't solid ground at all. It's just big chunks of denser stuff that floats on top of the mud like dumplings in a stew. But that was nothing compared to the other things—"

They had reached the vicinity of the salvage operation on Number Five dredge. To Kielland it looked like a huge cylinder-type vacuum cleaner with a number of flexible hoses sprouting from the top. The whole machine was three-quarters submerged in clinging mud. Off to the right a derrick floated hub-deep in slime; grapplers from it were clinging to the dredge and the derrick was heaving and splashing like a trapped hippopotamus. All about the submerged machine were Mud-pups, working like strange little beavers as the man supervising the operation wiped mud from his face and carried on a running line of shouts, curses, whistles and squeaks.

Suddenly one of the Mud-pups saw the newcomers. He let out a squeal, dropped his line in the mud and bounced up to the surface, dancing like a dervish on his broad webbed feet as he stared in unabashed curiosity. A dozen more followed his lead, squirming up and staring, shaking gobs of mud from their fur.

"No, *no!*" the man supervising the operation screamed. "*Pull,* you idiots. Come back here! Watch *out—*"

The derrick wobbled and let out a whine as steel cable sizzled out. Confused, the Mud-pups tore themselves away from the newcomers and turned back to their lines, but it was too late. Number Five dredge trembled, with a wet sucking sound, and settled back into the mud, blub—blub—blub.

The supervisor crawled down from his platform and sloshed across to where Simpson and Kielland were standing. He looked like a man who had suffered the torment of the damned for twenty minutes too long. "No more!" he screamed in Simpson's face. "That's all. I'm through. I'll pick up my pay any time you get it ready, and I'll finish off my contract at home, but I'm through here. One solid week I work to teach these idiots what I want them to do, and you have to come along at the one moment all week when I really need their concentration." He glared, his face purple. "Concentration! I should hope for so much! You got to have a brain to have concentration—"

"Barton, this is Kielland. He's here from the Home Office, to solve all our problems."

"You mean he brought us an evacuation ship?"

"No, he's going to tell us how to make this Installation pay. Right, Kielland?" Simpson's grin was something to see.

Kielland scowled. "What are you going to do with the dredge—just leave it there?" he asked angrily.

"No—I'm going to dig it out, again," said Barton, "after we take another week off to drum into those quarter-brained mud-hens just what it is we want them to do—again—and then persuade them to do it—again—and then hope against hope that nothing happens along to distract them—again. Any suggestions?"

Simpson shook his head. "Take a rest, Barton. Things will look brighter in the morning."

"Nothing ever looks brighter in the morning," said Barton, and he sloshed angrily off toward the Administration island.

"You see?" said Simpson. "Or do you want to look around some more?"

*

Back in Administration shack, Kielland sprayed his throat with Piper Fortified Bio-Static and took two tetracycline capsules from his samples case as he stared gloomily down at the little gob of blue-gray mud on the desk before him.

The Venusian bonanza, the sole object of the multi-million-dollar Piper Venusian Installation, didn't look like much. It ran in veins deep beneath the surface. The R&D men had struck it quite by accident in the first place, sampled it along with a dozen other kinds of Venusian mud—and found they had their hands on the richest 'mycin-bearing bacterial growth since the days of the New Jersey mud flats.

The value of the stuff was incalculable. Twenty-first century Earth had not realized the degree to which it depended upon its effective antibiotic products for maintenance of its health until the mutating immune bacterial strains began to outpace the development of new antibacterials. Early penicillin killed 96 per cent of all organisms in its spectrum—at first—but time and natural selection undid its work in three generations. Even the broad-spectrum drugs were losing their effectiveness to a dangerous degree within decades of their introduction. And the new drugs grown from Earth-born bacteria, or synthesized in the laboratories, were too few and too weak to meet the burgeoning demands of humanity—

Until Venus. The bacteria indigenous to that planet were alien to Earth—every attempt to transplant them had failed—but they grew with abandon in the warm mud currents of Venus. Not all mud was of value: only the singular blue-gray stuff that lay before Kielland on the desk could produce the 'mycin-like tetracycline derivative that was more powerful than the best of Earth-grown wide spectrum antibiotics, with few if any of the unfortunate side-effects of the Earth products.

The problem seemed simple: find the mud in sufficient quantities for mining, dredge it up, and transport it back to Earth to extract the drug. It was the first two steps of the operation that depended so heavily on the mud-acclimated natives of Venus for success. They were as much at home in the mud as they were in the dank, humid air above. They could distinguish one type of mud from another deep beneath the surface, and could carry a dredge-tube down to a lode of the blue-gray muck with the unfailing accuracy of a homing pigeon.

If they could only be made to understand just what they were expected to do. And that was where production ground down to a slow walk.

The next few days were a nightmare of frustration for Kielland as he observed with mounting horror the standard operating procedure of the Installation.

Men and Mud-pups went to work once again to drag Number Five dredge out of the mud. It took five days of explaining, repeating, coaxing and threatening to do it, but finally up it came—with mud caked and hardened in its insides until it could never be used again.

So they ferried Number Six down piecemeal from the special orbital transport ship that had brought it. Only three landing craft sank during the process, and within two weeks Simpson and Barton set

15

bravely off with their dull-witted cohorts to tackle the swamp with a spanking new piece of equipment. At last the delays were over—

Of course, it took another week to get the actual dredging started. The Mud-pups who had been taught the excavation procedure previously had either disappeared into the swamp or forgotten everything they'd ever been taught. Simpson had expected it, but it was enough to keep Kielland sleepless for three nights and drive his blood pressure to suicidal levels. At length, the blue-gray mud began billowing out of the dredge onto the platforms built to receive it, and the transport ship was notified to stand by for loading. But by the time the ferry had landed, the platform with the load had somehow drifted free of the island and required a week-long expedition into the hinterland to track it down. On the trip back they met a rainstorm that dissolved the blue-gray stuff into soup which ran out between the slats of the platform, and back into the mud again.

They did get the platform back, at any rate.

Meanwhile, the dredge began sucking up green stuff that smelled of sewage instead of the blue-gray clay they sought—so the natives dove mud-ward to explore the direction of the vein. One of them got caught in the suction tube, causing a three-day delay while engineers dismantled the dredge to get him out. In re-assembling, two of the dredge tubes got interlocked somehow, and the dredge burned out three generators trying to suck itself through itself, so to speak. That took another week to fix.

Kielland buried himself in the Administration shack, digging through the records, when the reign of confusion outside became too much to bear. He sent for Tarnier, the Installation physician, biologist, and erstwhile Venusian psychologist. Dr. Tarnier looked like the breathing soul of failure; Kielland had to steel himself to the wave of pity that swept through him at the sight of the man. "You're the one who tested these imbeciles originally?" he demanded.

Dr. Tarnier nodded. His face was seamed, his eyes lustreless. "I tested 'em. God help me, I tested 'em."

"How?"

"Standard procedures. Reaction times. Mazes. Conditioning. Language. Abstractions. Numbers. Associations. The works."

"Standard for Earthmen, I presume you mean."

"So what else? Piper didn't want to know if they were Einsteins or not. All they wanted was a passable level of intelligence. Give them natives with brains and they might have to pay them something. They thought they were getting a bargain."

"Some bargain."

"Yeah."

"Only your tests say they're intelligent. As intelligent, say, as a low-normal human being without benefit of any schooling or education. Right?"

"That's right," the doctor said wearily, as though he had been through this mill again and again. "Schooling and education don't enter into it at all, of course. All we measured was potential. But the results said they had it."

"Then how do you explain the mess we've got out there?"

"The tests were wrong. Or else they weren't applicable even on a basic level. Or something. I don't know. I don't even care much any more."

"Well I care, plenty. Do you realize how much those creatures are costing us? If we ever do get the finished product on the market, it'll cost too much for anybody to buy."

Dr. Tarnier spread his hands. "Don't blame me. Blame them."

"And then this so-called biological survey of yours," Kielland continued, warming to his subject. "From a scientific man, it's a prize. Anatomical description: limited because of absence of autopsy specimens. Apparently have endoskeleton, but organization of the internal organs remains obscure. Thought to be mammalianoid—there's a fence-sitter for you—but can't be certain of this because no young have been observed, nor any females in gestation. Extremely gregarious, curious, playful, irresponsible, etc.,

etc., etc. Habitat under natural conditions: uncertain. Diet: uncertain. Social organization: uncertain." Kielland threw down the paper with a snort. "In short, the only thing we're certain of is that they're here. Very helpful. Especially when every dime we have in this project depends on our teaching them how to count to three without help."

Dr. Tarnier spread his hands again. "Mr. Kielland, I'm a mere mortal. In order to measure something, it has to stay the same long enough to get it measured. In order to describe something, it has to hold still long enough to be observed. In order to form a logical opinion of a creature's mental capacity, it has to demonstrate some perceptible mental capacity to start with. You can't get very far studying a creature's habitat and social structure when most of its habitating goes on under twenty feet of mud."

"How about the language?"

"We get by with squeaks and whistles and sign language. A sort of pidgin-Venusian. They use a very complex system among themselves." The doctor paused, uncertainly. "Anyway, it's hard to get too tough with the Pups," he burst out finally. "They really seem to try hard—when they can just manage to keep their minds to it."

"Just stupid, carefree, happy-go-lucky kids, eh?"

Dr. Tarnier shrugged.

"Go away," said Kielland in disgust, and turned back to the reports with a sour taste in his mouth.

Later he called the Installation Comptroller. "What do you pay Mud-pups for their work?" he wanted to know.

"Nothing," said the Comptroller.

"*Nothing!*"

"We have nothing they can use. What would you give them—United Nations coin? They'd just try to eat it."

"How about something they *can* eat, then?"

"Everything we feed them they throw right back up. Planetary incompatibility."

"But there must be *something* you can use for wages," Kielland protested. "Something they want, something they'll work hard for."

"Well, they liked tobacco and pipes all right—but it interfered with their oxygen storage so they couldn't dive. That ruled out tobacco and pipes. They liked Turkish towels, too, but they spent all their time parading up and down in them and slaying the ladies and wouldn't work at all. That ruled out Turkish towels. They don't seem to care too much whether they're paid or not, though—as long as we're decent to them. They seem to like us, in a stupid sort of way."

"Just loving, affectionate, happy-go-lucky kids. I know. Go away." Kielland growled and turned back to the reports ... except that there weren't any more reports that he hadn't read a dozen times or more. Nothing that made sense, nothing that offered a lead. Millions of Piper dollars sunk into this project, and every one of them sitting there blinking at him expectantly.

For the first time he wondered if there really *was* any solution to the problem. Stumbling blocks had been met and removed before—that was Kielland's job, and he knew how to do it. But stupidity could be a stumbling block that was all but insurmountable.

Yet he couldn't throw off the nagging conviction that something more subtle than stupidity was involved....

Then Simpson came in, cursing and sputtering and bellowing for Louie. Louie came, and Simpson started dictating a message for relay to the transport ship. "Special order, rush, repeat, rush," Simpson grated. "For immediate delivery Piper Venusian Installation—one Piper Axis-Traction Dredge, previous specifications applicable—"

Kielland stared at him. "Again?"

Simpson gritted his teeth. "Again."

"Sunk?"

"Blub," said Simpson. "Blub, blub, blub."

Slowly, Kielland stood up, glaring first at Simpson, then at the little muddy creatures that were attempting to hide behind his waders, looking so forlorn and chastised and woebegone. "All right,"

Kielland said, after a pregnant pause. "That's all. You won't need to relay that order to the ship. Forget about Number Seven dredge. Just get your files in order and get a landing craft down here for me. The sooner the better."

Simpson's face lit up in pathetic eagerness. "You mean we're going to *leave?*"

"That's what I mean."

"The company's not going to like it—"

"The company ought to welcome us home with open arms," Kielland snarled. "They should shower us with kisses. They should do somersaults for joy that I'm not going to let them sink another half billion into the mud out here. They took a gamble and got cleaned, that's all. They'd be as stupid as your pals here if they kept coming back for more." He pulled on his waders, brushing penitent Mud-pups aside as he started for the door. "Send the natives back to their burrows or whatever they live in and get ready to close down. *I've* got to figure out some way to make a report to the Board that won't get us all fired."

He slammed out the door and started across to his quarters, waders going splat-splat in the mud. Half a dozen Mud-pups were following him. They seemed extraordinarily exuberant as they went diving and splashing in the mud. Kielland turned and roared at them, shaking his fist. They stopped short, then slunk off with their tails between their legs.

But even at that, their squeaking sounded strangely like laughter to Kielland....

In his quarters the light was so dim that he almost had his waders off before he saw the upheaval. The little room was splattered from top to bottom with mud. His bunk was coated with slime; the walls dripped blue-gray goo. Across the room his wardrobe doors hung open as three muddy creatures rooted industriously in the leather case on the floor.

Kielland let out a howl and threw himself across the room. *His samples case!* The Mud-pups scattered, squealing. Their hands were filled with capsules, and their muzzles were dripping with white powder. Two went between Kielland's legs and through the door. The third dove for the window with Kielland after him. The company man's hand closed on a slippery tail, and he fell headlong across the muddy bed as the culprit literally slipped through his fingers.

He sat up, wiping mud from his hair and surveying the damage. Bottles and boxes of medicaments were scattered all over the floor of the wardrobe, covered with mud but unopened. Only one large box had been torn apart, its contents ravaged.

Kielland stared at it as things began clicking into place in his mind. He walked to the door, stared out across the steaming gloomy mud flats toward the lighted windows of the Administration shack. Sometimes, he mused, a man can get so close to something that he can't see the obvious. He stared at the samples case again. Sometimes stupidity works both ways—and sometimes what looks like stupidity may really be something far more deadly.

He licked his lips and flipped the telephone-talker switch. After a misconnection or two he got Control Tower. Control Tower said yes, they had a small exploratory scooter on hand. Yes, it could be controlled on a beam and fitted with cameras. But of course it was special equipment, emergency use only—

He cut them off and buzzed Simpson excitedly. "Cancel all I said—about leaving. I mean. Change of plan. Something's come up. No, don't order anything—but get one of those natives that can understand your whistling and give him the word."

Simpson bellowed over the wire. "What word? What do you think you're doing?"

"I may just be saving our skins—we won't know for a while. But however you manage it, tell them we're definitely *not leaving Venus*. Tell them they're all fired—we don't want them around any more.

THE NATIVE SOIL

The Installation is off limits to them from here on in. And tell them we've devised a way to mine the lode without them—got that? Tell them the equipment will be arriving as soon as we can bring it down from the transport."

"Oh, now look—"

"You want me to repeat it?"

Simpson sighed. "All right. Fine. I'll tell them. Then what?"

"Then just don't bother me for a while. I'm going to be busy. Watching TV."

An hour later Kielland was in Control Tower, watching the pale screen as the little remote-controlled explorer circled the installation. Three TV cameras were in operation as he settled down behind the screen. He told Sparks what he wanted to do, and the ship whizzed off in the direction the Mud-pup raiders had taken.

At first, there was nothing but dreary mud flats sliding past the cameras' watchful eyes. Then they picked up a flicker of movement, and the ship circled in lower for a better view. It was a group of natives—a large group. There must have been fifty of them working busily in the mud, five miles away from the Piper Installation. They didn't look so carefree and happy-go-lucky now. They looked very much like desperately busy Mud-pups with a job on their hands, and they were so absorbed they didn't even see the small craft circling above them.

They worked in teams. Some were diving with small containers; some were handling lines attached to the containers; still others were carrying and dumping. They came up full, went down empty, came up full. The produce was heaped in a growing pile on a small semisolid island with a few scraggly trees on it. As they worked the pile grew and grew.

It took only a moment for Kielland to tell what they were doing. The color of the stuff was unmistakable. They were mining piles of blue-gray mud, just as fast as they could mine it.

With a gleam of satisfaction in his eye, Kielland snapped off the screen and nodded at Sparks to bring the cameras back. Then he rang Simpson again.

"Did you tell them?"

Simpson's voice was uneasy. "Yeah—yeah, I told them. They left in a hurry. Quite a hurry."

"Yes, I imagine they did. Where are your men now?"

"Out working on Number Six, trying to get it up."

"Better get them together and pack them over to Control Tower, fast," said Kielland. "I mean everybody. Every man in the Installation. We may have this thing just about tied up, if we can get out of here soon enough—"

Kielland's chair gave a sudden lurch and sailed across the room, smashing into the wall. With a yelp he tried to struggle up the sloping floor; it reared and heaved over the other way, throwing Kielland and Sparks to the other wall amid a heap of instruments. Through the windows they could see the gray mud flats careening wildly below them. It took only an instant to realize what was happening. Kielland shouted, "Let's get out of here!" and headed down the stairs, clinging to the railing for dear life.

Control Tower was sinking in the mud. They had moved faster than he had anticipated, Kielland thought, and snarled at himself all the way down to the landing platform below. He had hoped at least to have time to parley, to stop and discuss the whys and wherefores of the situation with the natives. Now it was abundantly clear that any whys and wherefores that were likely to be discussed would be discussed later.

And very possibly under twenty feet of mud—

A stream of men were floundering out of Administration shack, plowing through the mud with waders only half strapped on as the line of low buildings began shaking and sinking into the morass. From the direction of Number Six dredge another crew was heading for the Tower. But the Tower was rapidly growing shorter as the buoys that sustained it broke loose with ear-shattering crashes.

Kielland caught Sparks by the shoulder, shouting to be heard above the racket. "The transport—did you get it?"

"I—I think so."

"They're sending us a ferry?"

"It should be on its way."

Simpson sloshed up, his face heavy with dismay. "The dredges! They've cut loose the dredges."

"Bother the dredges. Get your men collected and into the shelters. We'll have a ship here any minute."

"But what's happening?"

"We're leaving—if we can make it before these carefree, happy-go-lucky kids here sink us in the mud, dredges, Control Tower and all."

Out of the gloom above there was a roar and a streak of murky yellow as the landing craft eased down through the haze. Only the top of Control Tower was out of the mud now. The Administration shack gave a lurch, sagging, as a dozen indistinct gray forms pulled and tugged at the supporting structure beneath it. Already a circle of natives was converging on the Earthmen as they gathered near the landing platform shelters.

"They're cutting loose the landing platform!" somebody wailed. One of the lines broke with a resounding snap, and the platform lurched. Then a dozen men dived through the mud to pull away the slippery, writhing natives as they worked to cut through the remaining guys. Moments later the landing craft was directly overhead and men and natives alike scattered as she sank down.

The platform splintered and jolted under her weight, began skidding, then held firm to the two guy ropes remaining. A horde of gray creatures hurled themselves on those lines as a hatchway opened above and a ladder dropped down. The men scurried up the ropes just as the plastic dome of the Control Tower sank with a gurgle.

Kielland and Simpson paused at the bottom of the ladder, blinking at the scene of devastation around them.

"Stupid, you say," said Kielland heavily. "Better get up there, or we'll go where Control Tower went."

"But—everything—gone!"

"Wrong again. Everything saved." Kielland urged the administrator up the ladder and sighed with relief as the hatch clanged shut. The jets bloomed and sprayed boiling mud far and wide as the landing craft lifted soggily out of the mire and roared for the clouds above.

Kielland wiped sweat from his forehead and sank back on his cot with a shudder. "*We* should be so stupid," he said.

"I must admit," he said later to a weary and mystified Simpson, "that I didn't expect them to move so fast. But when you've decided in your mind that somebody's really pretty stupid, it's hard to adjust to the idea that maybe he *isn't*, all of a sudden. We should have been much more suspicious of Dr. Tarnier's tests. It's true they weren't designed for Venusians, but they were designed to assess intelligence, and intelligence isn't a quality that's influenced by environment or species. It's either there or it isn't, and the good Doctor told us unequivocally that it was there."

"But their behavior."

"Even that should have tipped us off. There is a very fine line dividing incredible stupidity and incredible *stubbornness*. It's often a tough differential to make. I didn't spot it until I found them wolfing down the tetracycline capsules in my samples case. Then I began to see the implications. Those Mud-pups were stubbornly and tenaciously determined to drive the Piper Venusian Installation off Venus permanently, by fair means or foul. They didn't care how it got off—they just wanted it off."

"But why? We weren't hurting them. There's plenty of mud on Venus."

"Ah—but not so much of the blue-gray stuff we were after, perhaps. Suppose a space ship settled down in a wheatfield in Kansas along about harvest time and started loading wheat into the hold? I suppose the farmer wouldn't mind too much. After all, there's plenty of vegetation on Earth—"

"They're *growing* the stuff?"

"For all they're worth," said Kielland. "Lord knows what sort of metabolism uses tetracycline for food—but they are growing mud that yields an incredibly rich concentration of antibiotic ... their native food. They grow it, harvest it, live on it. Even the way they shake whenever they come out of the mud is a giveaway—what better way to seed their crop far and wide? We were mining away their staff of life, my friend. You really couldn't blame them for objecting."

"Well, if they think they can drive us off that way, they're going to have to get that brilliant intelligence of theirs into action," Simpson said ominously. "We'll bring enough equipment down there to mine them out of house and home."

"Why?" said Kielland. "After all, they're mining it themselves a lot more efficiently than we could ever do it. And with Piper warehouses back on Earth full of old, useless antibiotics that they can't sell for peanuts? No, I don't think we'll mine anything when a simple trade arrangement will do just as well." He sank back in his cot, staring dreamily through the port as the huge orbital transport loomed large ahead of them. He found his throat spray and dosed himself liberally in preparation for his return to civilization. "Of course, the natives are going to be wondering what kind of idiots they're dealing with to sell them pure refined extract of Venusian beefsteak in return for raw chunks of unrefined native soil. But I think we can afford to just let them wonder for a while."

www.ingramcontent.com/pod-product-compliance
Lightning Source LLC
Chambersburg PA
CBHW020349130626
46549CB00003B/1377